Disney's

A CHRISTMAS CAROL

THE MOVIE STORYBOOK

Disney's A CHRISTMAS CAROL

THE MOVIE STORYBOOK

Adapted by T.T. Sutherland
Based on the classic story by Charles Dickens
Based on the screenplay by Robert Zemeckis
Produced by Steve Starkey, Robert Zemeckis, Jack Rapke
Directed by Robert Zemeckis

For information address Disney Press, 114 Fifth Avenue, New York, New York 10011-5690.
Printed in the United States of America
First Edition
1 3 5 7 9 10 8 6 4 2
Library of Congress Catalog Card Number on f
ISBN 978-1-4231-2240-1

visit www.disneybooks.com
Disney.com/ChristmasCarol

Disney PRESS
New York

SUSTAINABLE
FORESTRY
INITIATIVE
Certified Chain of Custody
40% Certified Forests,
60% Certified Fiber Sourcing
www.sfiprogram.org
PWC-SFICOC-260

FOR TEXT PAPER ONLY

arley was dead, to begin with.
He lay in his coffin with his pale hands folded.
His business partner Ebenezer Scrooge glared coldly down
at the body. It was a poor, wretched funeral. There were no
mourners except Scrooge, and he did not look very sad. No
pain or grief passed across his face . . . until it came time to
pay the undertaker. Then Scrooge counted out three quid as
if each coin were being torn from his own flesh.

Ebenezer Scrooge was known throughout London as a
tight-fisted, mean old miser without a shred of sympathy or
warmth in his cold heart. And there was no time of the year
he hated more than Christmas.

Outside, lamplighters ran through the snowy cobblestoned streets, firing up the city's gas lamps. Candles glowed from the windows, and holly wreaths hung on the doors.

This was London in the year 1836. And it was Christmas Eve.

Scrooge stomped through the merry crowds with a horrible scowl on his face. Nobody spoke to him. The beggars did not dare ask him for pennies. Children ran the other way when they saw him coming. No one wished him a Merry Christmas.

This was how it was, and how it continued to be, for seven years following Jacob Marley's death. And then, on Christmas Eve, exactly seven years later . . . something new happened.

The evening began as usual, with Scrooge in his countinghouse. The weathered sign outside still read SCROOGE AND MARLEY. Scrooge was far too cheap to replace it. A thick fog rolled against the windows. Inside, Scrooge's clerk, Bob Cratchit, was huddled over his work, freezing. His teeth chattered, and his inkwell was so frozen he had to thaw the quill over a candle flame. Only a small lump of coal glowed in the hearth beside him. Across the hall, a fire crackled in Scrooge's fireplace, but Cratchit knew better than to ask for more coal.

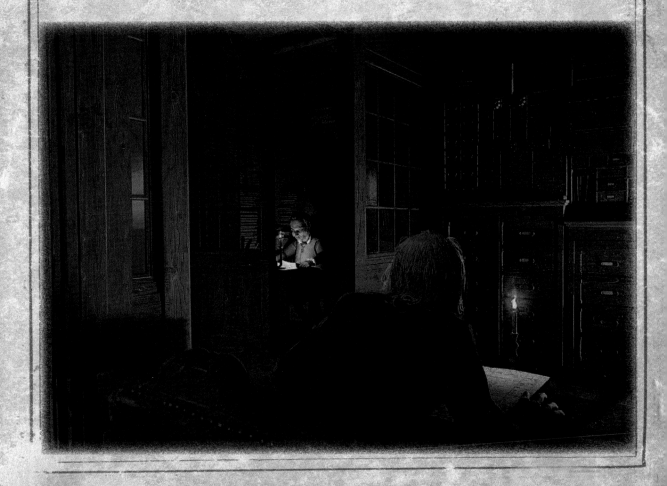

Suddenly, the office door swung open, and a cheerful voice boomed: "A Merry Christmas, uncle! God save you!"

Scrooge glared at his nephew Fred, a tall young man with sparkling eyes and red cheeks.

"Bah!" he answered. "Humbug!"

"Christmas a humbug?" Fred cried. "Uncle! You don't mean that!"

"'Merry Christmas,'" Scrooge grumbled. "What reason have *you* to be merry? You're poor enough."

"What right have you to be so dismal?" Fred shot back. "You're rich enough!"

Scrooge scowled even more ferociously.

"Humbug!" he snapped again. "If I could work my will, every idiot who goes about with 'Merry Christmas' on his lips should be boiled in his own pudding and buried with a stake of holly through his heart!"

Don't be angry, Uncle," Fred said charmingly. "Come! Dine with us tomorrow."

Scrooge's cold eyes turned even colder. "Good afternoon."

"Merry Christmas, Uncle!" Fred called as he backed out of the office.

"Good afternoon!" Scrooge shouted.

"And a Happy New Year!" Fred called before vanishing out the door.

The rest of the day's visitors did not fare any better. Two gentlemen stopped by looking for donations for the poor, only to be shouted at by an angry Scrooge. A tattered young boy knocked at the door, singing and shivering, only to be chased off by Scrooge in a rage.

Finally six o'clock came and Cratchit rose to leave. Scrooge fixed him with a fierce glare.

"You'll want all day tomorrow, I suppose?" he growled.

"If quite convenient, sir," Cratchit said politely, putting on his hat. "It's only once a year."

"It's not convenient, and it's not fair," Scrooge grumbled. "Be here all the earlier the next morning!"

Scrooge's house was tall and grand, but it had been neglected for many years, and it now looked dark and gloomy. Scrooge shuffled through the rusty gate and up the path, fumbling for his key. In the center of the front door was a large bronze knocker shaped like a simple orb. But as Scrooge reached to unlock the door, the knocker began to glow—and then Scrooge saw a terrifying sight. The knocker had turned into the face of his dead partner, Marley! His dead eyes were closed, as Scrooge had last seen them, and his face glowed in a sickly way.

Scrooge reached with trembling fingers to touch Marley's face. The eyes flew open! Scrooge shrieked and fell on the icy stoop. When he jumped back up again, the door knocker was once more an ordinary one.

Scrooge hurried inside, slammed the door and triple-locked it behind him. Surely it was just his imagination. He lit a candle and climbed the stairs, shivering as shadows gathered menacingly.

Upstairs, Scrooge bolted himself into his bed chamber, triple-locking this door as well. He changed into his nightgown and slippers and huddled in his armchair beside the tiny fire. He thought he saw Marley's face everywhere—in the shadows, in the tiles of the fireplace, in the flickering flames. And then, all of a sudden, Scrooge heard a horrible creaking sound. He froze, listening.

His front door was swinging open!

Scrooge stopped breathing. His heart pounded with terror. Someone was inside his house!

CLANK! CLANK! CLANK!

A rattling sound echoed through the house, as if someone were dragging heavy chains up the stairs.

Thump! Thump! Thump!

Footsteps! Someone was coming up the stairs and down the hall . . . closer and closer . . . toward Scrooge's chamber.

Scrooge shrank back in his chair, paralyzed with fear. The footsteps stopped right outside the door. There was a long moment of silence.

Crash! Clank! Slam! Blam!

A glowing, ghostly apparition, seven feet tall, sailed straight through the closed door.

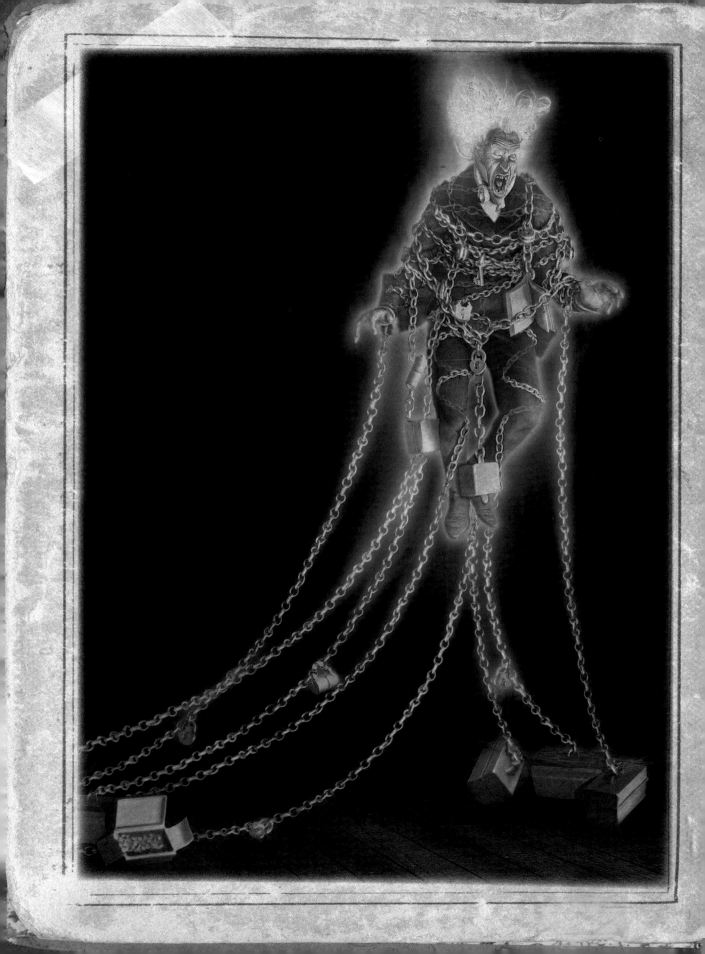

A heavy chain was wrapped around the ghost's middle, which was laden with huge cash boxes, keys, padlocks, ledgers, and purses—all of them made of ghostly steel. His pale eyes stared down at Ebenezer Scrooge.

"Who are you?" Scrooge asked, his voice trembling.

"In life I was your partner, Jacob Marley." The ghost let out a terrifying wail that shook the walls of the house. He towered over Scrooge, rattling his chains until Scrooge fell to his knees pleading for mercy.

"Dreadful apparition, why do you trouble me?" he cried in terror.

"I wear the chain I forged in life," Marley said. "I am here to warn you that you have yet a chance of escaping my fate. You will be haunted by three spirits . . . the Ghosts of Christmas Past, Present, and Future." He began to float toward the window. Scrooge's eyes widened as the window slowly swung open.

"Expect the first tomorrow, when the bell tolls one," Marley intoned. He drifted out the window. "Look to see me no more . . ." His voice faded.

Horrified, Scrooge slammed the window shut, raced across the room, and leaped into his bed, pulling the blanket over his head.

Sometime later, Scrooge awoke with a start. The room was dark and quiet. He blinked, listening. Had it all been a dream?

As if in answer, he heard the church bell outside toll once . . . and suddenly his bed curtains flew open! The room was filled with a blinding light. Scrooge shrank against the headboard, shielding his eyes. When he could see again, he realized the light was coming from the floor beside the bed. He peered over the edge of the mattress and saw a small, strange figure standing there. It looked like a child, but with the features of an old man.

A pure white light rose from his shoulders like a candle flame. His eyes gazed at Scrooge serenely.

"Are—are you the spirit whose coming was foretold to me?" Scrooge asked.

"I am," he said in a soft, gentle voice.

"Who and what are you?" Scrooge asked.

"I am the Ghost of Christmas Past," answered the spirit. "Your past." He seized Scrooge's arm in a surprisingly strong grip. "Rise! And walk with me!"

Another blast of light flooded the room. Blinking, Scrooge realized that night had turned to day outside . . . and that he was floating through the air toward the open window! He clutched at the spirit's arm as they flew out into the sky.

They were not over London anymore. A snowy country road had replaced the crowded, narrow streets of the city. Up ahead, a river wound under a bridge and past a small village.

Scrooge recognized the place with a start. "I was born here!"

The ghost brought Scrooge to an old, red-brick mansion.

"This was my school," Scrooge said, choking back tears.

"This school is not quite deserted," the spirit said. "A solitary child, neglected by his friends, is here still."

They flew through the cold entry hall and up a long, dark staircase to a classroom lined with empty desks. Alone in a corner, a boy sat reading. He was seven or eight years old. His face was full of sadness. It was young Ebenezer Scrooge himself.

"Let us see another Christmas," said the Ghost of Christmas Past, waving his hand. Around them, the plaster crumbled and cracks appeared across the windows. The younger version of Scrooge faded into the shadows. A new figure came in and walked between the desks.

This boy was seventeen years old. His hair was dark and lank, and his shoulders slumped gloomily. But he was still unmistakably Ebenezer Scrooge.

A little girl ran into the room after him and threw her arms around him. For the first time, a warmer look crossed the young man's face.

"My sister had a large heart," old Scrooge murmured softly.

"She died a woman . . . and had, as I think, children," said the spirit.

"One child," Scrooge said, thinking of his nephew Fred, his invitation to Christmas dinner, and how sternly Scrooge had turned him away.

As the shadows faded away, the ghost lifted him out
of the room and they flew low over a busy street crowded
with people and coaches. They were back in London on
another Christmas. Scrooge could not tell which one until
they arrived at a warehouse door. Painted above the door in
bright letters was the word FEZZIWIG!

"Do you know this place?" the ghost asked.

"Know it!" Scrooge said. "I was an apprentice here!" It was ten years later. Inside the warehouse, a jolly old man sat atop a tall desk, surveying the vast room.

"Why, it's old Fezziwig!" Scrooge said, delighted. He remembered his old master very well.

"Yo-ho there!" Fezziwig called, leaping off his desk. "Ebenezer! Dick!" The two apprentices dashed into the room. "No more work tonight! Christmas Eve! Clear away, my lads, and let's have lots of room here!" He clapped his hands and waved at the large room.

Dick and Ebenezer sprang into action, pushing tables aside. Time seemed to speed up as the room transformed into a merry ballroom, hung with lights and glowing with warmth. Christmas greenery hung from the ceiling, and the long table in the center of the room overflowed with a glorious feast.

The ghost looked at old Scrooge. "What's the matter?" the spirit asked.

"Nothing particular," Scrooge said, looking down at his hands. "Only . . . I should like to be able to say a word or two to my clerk just now. That's all." He remembered his last words with Cratchit and how unfeeling he had been about Christmas.

Old Scrooge and the ghost whirled around the room as it filled with young men and women dancing. The ghost drew Scrooge's attention to one couple in particular. It was young Ebenezer, and he was dancing with a pretty girl named Belle. He couldn't take his eyes off her . . . and neither could the older Scrooge.

Scrooge remembered this moment all too well. He looked away as the couple drew closer together. He did not want to relive the moment when he fell in love with beautiful Belle.

"My time grows short . . . " said the spirit. The light around his shoulders flared, and the two of them were transported to Scrooge's own countinghouse. It was five years later.

Young Ebenezer was sitting with Belle. She was still as beautiful as ever, but her eyes were full of tears. Ebenezer's face was not as hard as it would later become, but his eyes were greedy and restless.

"You've changed, Ebenezer," Belle was saying, brushing away tears. "Our contract is an old one. It was made when we were both poor and content to be so. When it was made . . . you were another man. Tell me, Ebenezer," she said, "if this contract had never been between us, would you seek me out now?"

Young Ebenezer did not reply, but Belle could see the answer in his eyes. She buried her face tearfully in her hands. "Ah, no!" she cried. "If you were free today, would you choose a girl left penniless by the death of her parents? You . . . who weighs everything by gain."

He turned away from her, bowing his head.

"I release you, Ebenezer," Belle said, standing up. "May you be happy in the life you have chosen."

And with those words, she walked out of his life.

Old Scrooge turned to the ghost with tears running down his face. "*Remove me!*" he begged. "I cannot bear it!" He lunged at the ghost, seizing the spirit's cap and shoving it over his head to hide his flame. But the light could not be forced down, and with a bright explosion, the cap blasted Scrooge into the air!

Hanging on for dear life, Scrooge found himself flying up toward the moon and stars. He tried to cling to the cap and the light, but all at once they vanished. The ghost was gone! Scrooge began falling—straight down to the ground!

He screamed as he fell. London grew closer and closer below him. He could see the Thames River and the dome of St. Paul's, and then, rushing toward him, he saw his own house. He was hurtling right down onto the roof!

Scrooge clamped his eyes shut, certain he was about to die.

THUD!

Scrooge hit the floor of his bedchamber. He staggered to his feet and fell into his bed, rubbing his sore head. Almost at once, he heard a loud *BONG!*, like the bell that had announced the first ghost.

Another ghost was coming! Scrooge tried to hide under the covers, but with a violent jolt, his bed suddenly slid across the floor. It jerked to a stop in the doorway and dropped him on the threshold of his sitting room.

Scrooge squinted into a glowing red light. The room looked unnaturally huge. The ceiling yawned high above him, and tall windows ran along the side of the room. Every inch of the space was decorated for Christmas.

And right in the center of the room . . . was the Ghost of Christmas Present.

This ghost was a huge, jolly giant. He sat beside
a crackling fire on an enormous throne made of food:
turkeys, geese, suckling pigs, wreaths of sausage, mince pies,
plum puddings, gleaming red apples, juicy oranges, and
steaming bowls of punch—everything one could wish for at
a Christmas feast.

The ghost held a burning torch and wore a green robe
trimmed with white fur. A holly wreath sat on top of his
long, dark brown curls. He radiated good cheer.

"Touch my robe!" the spirit commanded. Scrooge did as
he was told, and the ghost tipped his torch toward the floor.
Instantly the floorboards became transparent, as if they had
turned to glass.

Scrooge leaped back, alarmed, but the floor held firm beneath his feet. To his surprise, the entire room began to rise—higher and higher, sliding out of the house until it was floating over the city street.

It was a bright, sunny winter morning outside, with a cheerful white blanket of snow covering London. Everyone called out "Merry Christmas" to one another as they passed by. The ghost chuckled at the peaceful joy below them. Wherever he saw a quarrel begin, he sprinkled magic dust, and the quarrelers began to smile and laugh, forgetting why they were angry.

The ghost steered them into a narrow street lined
with red-brick houses, all of them exactly alike—dirty and
crumbling. He stopped above one in particular. Scrooge
wrinkled his nose at the poor surroundings.

The spirit smiled wryly. "'Tis all your loyal clerk can
afford for his meager fifteen bob a week."

Scrooge realized with surprise that this must be Bob Cratchit's house. The ghost took him inside so they could see the cramped room where the large Cratchit family was gathered, preparing for Christmas dinner.

Scrooge's clerk was carrying a young boy on his shoulder—his youngest son, known as Tiny Tim. Tim was small and frail for his six years, but he smiled sweetly at all of them. He carried a tiny wooden crutch and wore iron braces on his legs. Bob handed him gently down to the floor and sent him off to wash up.

"How did little Tim behave at church?" his wife asked him.

"Good as gold . . . and better," Bob answered. His wife and daughter both had tears in their eyes. Bob's voice trembled as he went on. "I—I believe he grows stronger and more hearty every day, my dear."

They nodded, but Scrooge could see they did not fully believe it. Tim was very ill.

Scrooge brushed away a tear as Bob reached for the hand of his youngest son. "Kind spirit," said Scrooge, "say Tiny Tim will be spared."

"If these shadows remain unaltered by the future," said the spirit, "the child will die."

Scrooge was too shaken to speak as their room rose slowly out of the Cratchit house and the Ghost of Christmas Present steered them away.

At last the spirit set them down in a parlor familiar to Scrooge: this was the home of his nephew Fred. Fred and his wife and half a dozen friends were laughing over a guessing game called yes and no.

"You're thinking of an animal," said Fred's friend Topper.

"Yes," said Fred.

"A rather disagreeable animal," Fred's wife guessed.

"Yes."

"Who lives in London?" said another guest.

"Yes!" Fred said.

"A horse!" guessed one.

"A cow!" guessed another.

"No," Fred answered, shaking his head.

"I know what it is, Fred!" cried his sister-in-law. "I know! It's your Uncle Scroooooooge!"

"YES!" Fred shouted, and everyone began laughing. Scrooge tried to look away, but the Ghost forced him to watch.

"I'm sorry for him," said Fred. "Who suffers from his ill whims? Only himself. He decides to dislike us and won't

come and dine with us . . . and what's the consequence?
He loses a dinner!"

"Indeed, he loses a *very good* dinner!" his wife announced,
causing another round of laughter.

"He's certainly given us plenty of merriment, that's
for sure," Fred said, raising his glass. "And it would be
ungrateful not to drink to his health. A Merry Christmas
to the old man! To Uncle Scrooge!"

The scene faded as everyone lifted their glasses, and Scrooge found himself inside a huge clockworks with the ghost. All around him, enormous gears and counterweights moved. He could see the vast glass clock face as if he were inside it. The time was one minute to midnight.

Scrooge realized that the torch was beginning to flicker and die. The spirit was much, much older now. His hair was completely gray, and his face was gaunt and wrinkled.

"My life upon this globe is very brief," said the ghost. "It ends tonight at midnight. Hark! The time is drawing near."

The clock began to toll. BONG! BONG! BONG! With every strike, the chamber reverberated terribly. Scrooge clamped his hands over his ears and watched in horror as the Ghost of Christmas Present dissolved into sparkling dust.

The dust scattered, lifted away by a ghostly wind, and Scrooge was left alone in the dark chamber. The last vibrations of the clock bell reverberated around him. He lowered his hands and saw a menacing figure wrapped in a black hooded cape.

Scrooge could see no face inside the hood. The shape was grave and silent.

Scrooge dropped to his knees and clasped his hands, trembling with fear. "Am I . . . am I in the presence of the Ghost of Christmas Yet to Come?"

The shadow did not reply.

"You are about to show me shadows of the things that have not happened . . . but *will* happen. Is that so, spirit?"

Still there was no answer.

"Ghost of the Future!" Scrooge cried. "I fear you more than any specter I have seen! But I am prepared. Lead on."

All at once, the phantom lunged at Scrooge! Scrooge reeled backward and found himself falling down a long, steep staircase. His head cracked painfully on the stone stairs as he tumbled head over heels, finally landing at the entrance to the Royal Exchange.

It was late afternoon, another Christmas. Three well-dressed businessmen were standing on the steps conversing. They took no notice of Scrooge lying in the snow below them.

"When did he die?" asked one.

"Last night, I believe," said another, "or sometime on Christmas Day."

"I thought he'd never die," said the third. "What's he done with his money?"

"He hasn't left it to *me*," said the first with a yawn. "That's all I know." The others laughed.

"It's likely to be a cheap funeral," the third man said. "For the life of me, I don't know anyone who'd go to it."

The men laughed and soon vanished. Scrooge climbed to his feet and saw that the light had changed. It was evening. The spirit rose up beside him. Silently it pointed with a long, ghostly finger. Full of foreboding, Scrooge turned to look . . . and saw a hearse waiting at the other end of the street.

It was the same dark carriage that had carried away the body of Jacob Marley. Two black horses stamped menacingly between the braces. Scrooge stepped back, shaking with horror. Suddenly the phantom shadow whipped around . . . and pointed right at Scrooge!

The dark stallions charged! Scrooge ran for his life, but his slippers skidded on the icy snow and he slid over the cobblestones. Behind him, the hearse thundered closer and closer. He was going to be crushed beneath the horses' massive hooves!

As he ran, Scrooge realized with a bolt of terror that he was shrinking. Around him, the houses were getting taller, the cobblestones bigger and bigger. Still the hearse chased him. The deafening clatter of the horses' hooves echoed off the walls like thunder.

When he was the size of a mouse, Scrooge dove into a drainpipe, trying to escape. He held his breath as the water swirled and surged around him. The pipe spit him out into the open air and he found himself on an icy rooftop, sliding head over heels down the steep incline. With a shout of terror, he plummeted over the edge and fell to the cold, hard street below.

On the street was an old, tottering woman carrying a heavy bundle over her shoulder. With a thud, Scrooge landed in the bundle of rags on the woman's back. Now the size of a thimble,

he flailed in the musty fabric, trying to see. He heard the creak of a shop door opening and closing behind her.

It was a rag-and-bone shop, where old rags were bought and sold. Scrooge tumbled onto the floor as the woman dumped out her bundle. In the firelight, he could see his shadow on the wall . . . and beside it, the vast, menacing shadow of the specter.

The woman was talking to the shop owner about taking the bed curtains from a dead man's bed. She pulled out a shirt and shoved it at him. "Here. It's the best he had, and they'd have wasted it, if it hadn't been for me!"

Scrooge peered up at the shirt. It looked horribly familiar.

"Somebody was fool enough to put it on him to be buried in, ha ha!" she went on. "But I took it off again and dressed him in an old calico one! Ha ha!" She shook her head. "He frightened everyone away when he was alive. If he had somebody to look after him when he was struck with Death, instead of lying there, gasping out his last breath all alone . . . we'd never have these things to sell."

Scrooge turned to the spirit and clasped his hands beseechingly.

"Spirit!" he cried. "I see! *I see!* The case of this unhappy man, who dies a solitary, lonesome death, might be my own. My life tends that way now. . . ."

The spirit's spectral hand floated down—and seized him!

When Scrooge opened his eyes again, he was standing in a nearly bare chamber. A shaft of light illuminated the body of a man lying on a bed, motionless under a ragged sheet.

Scrooge was back to normal size again. Still in eerie silence, the phantom lifted its hand . . . and pointed at the bed.

Scrooge shook his head and backed away.

"Spirit!" he begged. "This is a fearful place! When I leave it, I shall not leave its lesson. Trust me."

The spirit kept reaching out, extending its finger until it touched the man's head.

"Please," said Scrooge, "let me see some tenderness connected with a death, or this dark chamber will forever haunt me!"

Instantly the room changed . . . and Scrooge found himself standing inside Bob Cratchit's house. The family, quiet and somber, was seated around the hearth.

"It's late," said Mrs. Cratchit. "It's past your father's time."

"He's walked slower these last few evenings," Peter said.

"He has walked with Tiny Tim on his shoulder, fast indeed," said Mrs. Cratchit. "But he was very light to carry . . . and your father loved him so."

Bob Cratchit came in, and the children rushed to him.

His face was worn and older than before, and he moved with heavy sadness.

"You went today, then?" Mrs. Cratchit asked.

"Yes, my dear," Bob said as he sat down by the fire. "I wish you could have gone. It would have done you good to see how green a place it is. But you'll see it often. I promised him that I would walk there every Sunday." His voice broke, and he began to weep. "Oh, my child . . . my little child."

Scrooge bowed his head.

"Specter," he said quietly, "something tells me our parting moment is at hand. Tell me . . . who was that man . . . we saw lying dead?"

A violent wind tore through the room, ripping apart the walls and sending them flying off into space. After a loud, furious few moments, the dust cleared, and Scrooge found himself in a dark, desolate churchyard at night. A gloomy wind howled around the gravestones. Scrooge stood alone on the frozen snow.

The phantom lifted one bony hand and pointed to a nearby gravestone overrun with weeds.

Scrooge hesitated. "Before I draw nearer," he said, "answer me one question. Are these the shadows of things that *will* be . . . or shadows of things that *may* be?"

The ghost did not speak. It dropped its arm, and in a flash of moonlight, the name on the gravestone became clear: EBENEZER SCROOGE.

Scrooge dropped to his knees and cried out. "Am I that man who lies upon the bed?"

The phantom swung its finger from the grave to Scrooge and back again.

"Spirit!" Scrooge cried desperately. "Hear me! I'm not the man I was! Why show me this if I'm past all hope? Good

spirit, assure me that I may change these shadows you have shown me!" He jumped up to run, and his feet sank into the grave. It was pulling him in—the grave was swallowing him alive!

"Help me, spirit!" Scrooge shouted. "I will honor Christmas in my heart and try to keep it all the year. Oh, pray, spirit! Tell me I may sponge away the writing on that stone!"

The grave crumbled into a pit and Scrooge fell into the hole, falling past dark earth walls and toward the open coffin at the bottom. He closed his eyes just before impact and . . .

Whump!

He jolted to an abrupt stop.

Scrooge opened his eyes. There was wood below him . . . but it was not a coffin. It was his own bedroom floor!

With a joyous yelp, Scrooge untangled himself and leaped to his feet. He threw his arms around the bed curtains and cried out. "They're here! They're still here! I'M STILL HERE!" He began dancing around the room, and then noticed that it was daylight outside.

Joyfully, he ran to the window and threw it open. Golden sunlight sparkled across the snowy street. Church bells sang out in the distance. Scrooge breathed in the cold, crisp air. He was alive!

Below him, a young boy was pulling a sled through the snow.

"What's today, my fine fellow?" Scrooge called down.

"Today?" the boy answered. "Why, Christmas Day!"

"It's Christmas Day!" Scrooge sang out. "I haven't missed it! The spirits have done it all in one night!" He called down to the boy again. "Hallo, my fine fellow! Do you know the poulterer's on the corner? Do you know whether they've sold the prize turkey that was hanging there?"

"The one as big as me?" asked the boy. "It's hanging there now."

"Is it?" Scrooge said. "Go and buy it! Bring it here, and I'll give you a shilling . . . come back in less than five minutes, and I'll give you half a crown!"

The boy flew off like a shot. Scrooge rubbed his hands in delight. "I'll send it to Bob Cratchit. He shan't know who sent it . . . it's twice the size of Tiny Tim!"

Scrooge practically flew down the stairs, singing and laughing. He threw open the front door and shouted: "MERRY CHRISTMAS!" into the street. He kissed his door knocker, remembering the face of Jacob Marley, which had begun his ghostly adventure. When the boy came struggling back with the poulterer and the turkey, Scrooge paid for a carriage to take them to the Cratchits'. And then he set off down the street to church, dressed in his best clothes, calling out Christmas greetings to everyone he saw and dropping coins in the carolers' cups.

That night, he went to his nephew Fred's. He was nervous that he would not be welcome—but Fred's wife gave him a warm hug, and Fred shook his hand so vigorously Scrooge nearly fell over. There was wonderful food and lots of laughter, and Ebenezer Scrooge had a very merry Christmas indeed.

The next morning, Bob Cratchit was sixteen minutes late to work. He slunk in and hurried over to his desk, but Scrooge was watching for him.

"Cratchit!" he bellowed from his office. "What do you mean by coming here at this time of day?"

"I—I'm very sorry, sir," Bob said, coming to Scrooge's door.

"I am not going to stand for this sort of thing any longer!" Scrooge shouted. "And therefore . . . I'm about to RAISE YOUR SALARY!" He started laughing.

Bob Cratchit could not believe his ears. Had his master gone mad? What had happened to miserly old Mr. Scrooge?

"A Merry Christmas, Bob," Scrooge said, clapping him on the back. "A merrier Christmas than I've given you in many a year! I'll raise your salary, and do whatever I can to help your struggling family." He poured coins into Bob's hands and sent him out to buy more coal to warm the office.

Walking past the window, still in shock, Bob glanced in and saw the strangest sight.

Mr. Scrooge was *dancing*!